The Case of the Missing Emeralds

(A Cody Smith Mystery)

by Dorothy Francis

Cover and Inside Illustrations: William Ersland

About the Author

Dorothy Francis has written many books and stories for children and adults.

Ms. Francis holds a bachelor of music degree from the University of Kansas. She has traveled with an all-girl dance band, taught music in public and private schools, and served as a correspondence teacher for the Institute of Children's Literature in Connecticut.

She and her husband, Richard, divide their time between Marshalltown, Iowa, and Big Pine Key, Florida.

Printed in the United States of America. For information, contact

Perfection Learning® Corporation

1000 North Second Avenue, P.O. Box 500

Logan, Iowa 51546-0500

Phone: 800-831-4190 • Fax: 712-644-2392

Paperback ISBN 0-7891-5230-4

Cover Craft® ISBN 0-7807-9653-5

Printed in the U.S.A.

Table of Contents

1

Goldfinch Farm

My name is Cody Smith. I used to live in New York City. But right now, I'm stuck at an Iowa rest stop.

It's hot. Sweat stings my eyes. I imagine freckles popping out on my face like bran flakes. But I like the clean smell of the air.

It was my fault Mom and Maria drove off without me. I should have told them I was getting out to look at the historical marker.

Our luggage was piled high. And they couldn't see I was gone. Drat! I hated sitting here alone.

I studied the marker. I touched the hot bronze letters. Then I read the words.

LOUIS JOLIET and JACQUES MARQUETTE entered the Iowa River on the 25th of June 1673. They explored what later became Iowa soil. This is the place...

"This is the place," I whispered. Those guys really grabbed some fame. Cool, I thought.

I tried for fame earlier this summer. I wanted to earn a listing in the *Guinness Book of World Records*. I planned to wear the same Band-Aid for a hundred days. But after three days, I took it off.

Then I tried finding Bigfoot in New York City. That was bad thinking. I was still not famous.

I had wanted to impress Dad. He deserted us. He just walked out. But I've given up on impressing him. He's the loser, not us.

Now I just wanted to do something worthwhile. Something people would notice.

How about getting my name on a bronze marker? I thought.

"The Cody Smith Trail," I said. I liked the sound of that. "The Cody Smith River. Cody Smith's Peak."

I was still trying out the words when Mom arrived. Was I ever glad to see her and Maria!

"Cody!" Mom called. "You scared us! Get in the car!"

"LOST BOY FOUND." Maria blurted the words and fluffed her black curls. She planned to be a reporter someday. She liked to practice creating headlines.

"I'm sorry, Mom." I glared at Maria. She grinned. Then she blew her cinnamon-ball breath at me.

Maria Romero was spending the summer with us. Her parents were working in Italy. She was bossy, but I liked her anyway.

Mom sighed. She held her slim figure stiff like a Popsicle. Then she relaxed.

"It's okay, Cody," Mom said. "I'm just glad you're safe."

We drove all afternoon. We stopped a few times to stretch our legs. I made sure not to get left behind again.

I was sick of sitting in the hot car. Finally, Mom said, "We'll reach Goldfinch Farm soon. But before we do, we need to talk."

THE CASE OF THE MISSING EMERALDS

I braced myself for bad news. Mom meant business when she used her store-detective voice. She seldom used it now. She had been downsized from her detective job in New York.

That's why we were going to visit Gram for the rest of the summer. We'd be staying with her until Mom found a new job.

"I need to share some secrets about your grandmother," Mom said. "And about the farm."

"Secrets?" I asked. I hadn't seen Gram Cornwall since I was four. But sometimes we exchanged email messages. "What's up, Mom?"

"My mother's a recluse," Mom said. "She never leaves the farm. Nobody comes to visit. The hired man, Kaleb Webster, works the land. He runs her errands."

"He lives there?" I asked.

"Yes," Mom said. "He and his grandson, Finn, have their own cottage."

I couldn't imagine anyone never leaving home.

"My mother's parents died when she was a baby," Mom said. "She lived on Goldfinch Farm with her grandparents. They were very old. Her grandfather was the captain of a Missouri River steamboat. One day, the River Queen hit a submerged tree. The boat sank. But everyone survived."

"SHIPWRECK! EVERYONE SAVED!"

We ignored Maria's headline.

"The captain saved the boat's furnishings," Mom

said. "But one of the families onboard, the Glockners, lost an emerald necklace. They accused him of stealing it."

"Did he?" I asked.

"Nobody knows," Mom said. "But the scandal ruined our family's reputation. My mother eventually married. She and Dad lived on the farm. But people snubbed them. Mother wouldn't leave Goldfinch Farm even after Dad died. She thought leaving would make her look guilty. She still believes that after all these years."

"Maybe Maria and I can find the emeralds," I said.

"They're probably on the river bottom," Mom said. "Anyway, I want you and Maria to be emissaries. Go-betweens. I want you to be friendly kids reaching out to people in River Bluffs."

"I'd rather find emeralds," I said. "A guy never knows what he can do until he tries. Mom, finding those emeralds would help Gram. It would be a worthwhile mystery to solve."

I imagined a bronze marker. THE CODY SMITH TREASURE. This was the spot where . . . I didn't blurt out the words. That would sound too much like Maria.

"Forget about emeralds, Cody," Mom said. She turned off the highway. "Help me count miles. Each crossroad marks a mile. The crossroads divide the land into sections of 160 acres. Let's count five crossroads."

Mom turned when Maria and I shouted, "FIVE!"

"There's the Benson place," Mom said. "The only other house on this section will be Goldfinch Farm."

My throat tightened when I saw the farm. I felt as if I had swallowed a whole marshmallow.

Thistles clogged the lane. The house hid behind a thorn hedge. Weeds scraped the underside of our car.

"Graveyard Manor," I whispered. "Mom, this is spooky. I'm not sure I want to go any farther."

"There's nothing to worry about," Mom assured me. "It's just a little overgrown. Kaleb must be getting too old to care for it properly."

Stone pillars rose on either side of the driveway. A tangle of weeds almost hid the faded sign: GOLDFINCH FARM. The branches scraping the sides of the car were like clutching fingers.

"RELATIVES VISIT SPOOK HOUSE," Maria said.

"Tomorrow I'll do some weeding and trimming," Mom said.

A red rooster strutted to join three hens on the porch. Then a tall, slim woman opened the door. I had expected a silver-haired lady in a housedress and apron. Wasn't that what grandmothers looked like? Had strangers moved in?

I stared at the red-haired woman. She wore designer jeans. Her lime green sneakers matched her T-shirt. Wrinkles wreathed her mouth and cheeks. But her blue eyes sparkled like a teenager's.

Gram Cornwall rushed to hug us. "Welcome! Welcome!"

Once we stepped inside the house, I gasped. It was like a palace. It glowed. And it smelled of freshly baked bread.

Glittering chandeliers hung from the ceilings. Wine-colored carpets felt like foam under our feet. Polished furniture gleamed in all the rooms.

And that wasn't all. Walnut paneling lined the walls. And lace curtains hung at the windows.

"Cool, Gram!" I said. "This is some neat house!"

"We'll explore the house later," Gram said. "Let's unpack your car."

Everyone carried stuff inside. Gram led the way up a curving walnut staircase. She showed us to our rooms.

I plunked my suitcase beside a brass bed. I looked around. Then I pulled a book from a walnut bookcase.

Opening it, I read the name scrawled inside. Cody Cornwall. How could that be? Then I realized this room had once belonged to my uncle.

Another shelf held an Indian arrowhead collection. Wow! I touched the sharp, flinty points. I wished I'd known Uncle Cody.

I unpacked quickly. Then I hurried downstairs.

The dining room table was set for six. "Kaleb and Finn will join us," Gram said.

Kaleb arrived soon. He wore a blue workshirt under bib overalls. And he smelled like spearmint.

He had a two-toned head and face. It was strange. The top half was bald and white. The bottom half was deeply tanned. Then I realized that Kaleb must wear a hat outside.

I liked to nickname people. But Kaleb's old-fashioned name fit him perfectly. So I didn't give him a nickname.

"Where's Finn?" Gram asked.

Kaleb flushed a brick red as he spoke. "He's busy, Mrs. Cornwall. He's taking care of his calf's injured leg."

My mind whirled. Why would Kaleb feel embarrassed about Finn? Maybe Finn didn't want to meet us.

2

A Scream in the Morning

I tried not to stare at the soup Gram served. It was bright orange and sprinkled with black pepper.

"Chilled carrot soup," Gram said. "A true health food! It's page four in my soup cookbook. And it's perfect for a hot Iowa evening. Enjoy!"

Eat it, Cody. Be polite, I thought to myself. I saw Maria pop a cinnamon ball into her mouth. She grinned at me.

Gram had monster-size soupspoons. The thick goop clung like orange mud to the cold silver. But I took a bite.

"It's great, Gram," I said. Did God forgive white lies? "I didn't know you wrote cookbooks."

"Carrot soup's in my third book," Gram said. "I'm working alphabetically. *The Amazing Artichoke* is first."

Artichoke? I changed the subject quickly. "That's a cool brass bed in my room, Gram. I've never seen one like it before."

"It survived the sinking of the River Queen," Gram explained.

"Was that the boat your grandfather was the captain of?" I asked.

"Yes, it was. My grandfather saved all of our furniture when the River Queen went down," Gram said. "That started many problems. People thought Grandfather found the Glockners' necklace. Folks believed he sold it. They thought he used the money to furnish our house."

"But wasn't the boat's furniture wet and ruined?" Maria asked.

"The boat only sank to the cabin deck," Gram said. "The furniture remained dry."

"Maybe Maria and I can find those emeralds," I said. "Wouldn't that be awesome?"

"Your Uncle Cody looked for that necklace before he died," Gram said. "But he never found it."

"I saw his arrowhead collection," I said. "Where did he find those?"

"Right here on Goldfinch Farm," Gram said. "Indians lived on this land ages ago. There's a college professor camping by the river this summer. He's an archaeologist from a nearby university. He's here to gather material on Indians for a book."

"Do you still have pictures of the River Queen?" Mom asked.

"Yes," Gram said. "We'll look at them after supper."

I finished my soup. Had it turned my teeth orange? I bit into my sandwich. I looked for orange teeth marks on the bread. There weren't any.

But now my mouth burned. And my eyes watered. Yikes!

"Radish sandwich filling," Gram said. "The recipe will be in *Rousing Radishes* when I reach the Rs."

I drank two glasses of water. So did Mom. And Maria.

After supper, Kaleb returned to his cottage. Gram brought out a velvet-covered album. I inhaled the musty smell of old paper. Gram turned the yellowed pages carefully. There were pictures of the River Queen.

15

...m, that steamboat's really something!" I said.
...t black smokestack is cool. And look at that paddle
...heel. Awesome! I wish I could have sailed on it."

Then Gram reached pictures of my Uncle Cody. I studied them carefully.

"You look a lot like your uncle," Gram said. "I'm sorry you never knew him."

When I turned a page, a paper fell out. I picked it up.

"Gram!" I said. "A map! Maybe it's a treasure map. Maybe it'll lead to the missing emeralds."

"I'm afraid not, Cody," Gram said. "The police found the map in your uncle's billfold. The night of his car crash. They tried to follow the map. They found nothing."

"Could I copy it?" I asked. "Maybe they overlooked something."

Gram brought paper and a ballpoint pen. "Looking for treasure will help pass the time, I suppose," she said.

That night we all went to bed early. I wanted to think about treasure hunting. But I fell asleep.

((((((

The next morning, Kaleb arrived for breakfast. He was alone. Didn't Finn ever get hungry?

Gram served apricot pancakes. Double awesome! I

16

guessed Gram's A cookbook might be my favorite. I tried to forget artichokes.

"Why don't you kids explore this morning?" Gram suggested. "Maybe you'll see Finn in the barn. He keeps his calf there."

Maria and I ran outside. "Let's find those emeralds," I said. "We'll search places others overlooked."

"KIDS FIND EMERALDS," Maria said. "Okay, Cody. But first let's explore the farm. What's this?" She pointed to a low, slanting door near the back porch.

"That's the storm cellar," I said. "Mom told me. If there's a storm, everyone runs here."

Sometimes Maria thought she knew everything. I liked it when I could tell her stuff.

I lifted the door. We crept down earthen steps.

Maria's eyes grew as wide as donut holes. "What a creepy place."

"Mom says Gram cans garden vegetables," I said. "She stores them here. I'd hate to be stuck here during a storm. It's dank. It's dark. And it smells bad. I hate bad smells in my lungs."

We hurried back outside. "Hey, look at that round, brick tower. It's a silo," I explained. "Kaleb stores corn there."

We walked on to the chicken yard. A sagging wire fence surrounded a weathered shed. White hens scattered like giant snowflakes.

Then a red rooster zoomed toward me. It clucked. It pecked my ankles. Yikes! Gram didn't warn us she had an attack rooster!

"Shoo!" I shouted and backed off. Maria laughed. But she backed off too.

"ROOSTER RAGE SCARES CITY KIDS," Maria said.

We headed to a pine grove. "Wonder what's beyond the trees?" I asked. "Maybe there's a path to the river."

"Your grandmother said to stay away from the river," Maria warned.

"We might just accidentally wander to it," I said. I pulled Maria along.

Deep shadows filled the grove. We slipped on pine needles underfoot. The pine smell reminded me of Christmas. It was a neat smell.

"What's wrong?" Maria asked when I stopped. "Maybe we should turn back."

"Look to our left," I said. "I think I saw someone duck behind a pine."

I peered into the shadows. Nothing moved.

"I'm out of here," Maria said.

But just then we reached a clearing. A man called out.

"Hey, kids, it's okay. I'm Professor Bidwell. Your grandmother said you might come visiting."

We stepped across a small creek.

"I'm Cody Smith," I said. "And this is Maria Romero."

I studied the tall man dressed in khaki shirt and pants. He was sitting in a camp chair. And he held a laptop computer.

I smelled wood smoke on his clothes. A campfire smoldered near his tent.

"Name's Smith, huh?" The professor smiled.

"That's right," I said. Was this guy teasing me? It bugs me when people tease me about my common name.

"Everyone in the world used to be named Smith," I said. Maria sighed. She'd heard my story before.

"When a Smith did something wrong," I said, "the other Smiths punished him. They made him change his name. There are hardly any of us Smiths left anymore."

Professor Bidwell laughed. "I like your name, Cody. You see, my name's Smith too. Professor R. Smith Bidwell."

I relaxed. Smitty was an okay guy. I nicknamed him immediately. The Smiths of the world should stick together.

"You're studying about Indians?" I asked.

"Long-ago Indians," Smitty said. "They camped here close to the river."

We listened to Smitty for a while. Then we headed back to the house.

"Maybe he's a crook searching for the emeralds,"

Maria whispered. "PHONY PROFESSOR FINDS EMERALDS."

Why hadn't I thought of that? It bugged me when Maria came up with good ideas before I did.

I was thinking about that when we heard a scream. Then all was silent.

Maria and I looked at each other. Then we sprinted for the barn.

3

Finn Webster

"Duck into the barn!" I yelled. I pulled Maria behind me.

"Why would anyone be screaming?" Maria asked. "Cody! I'm scared."

I blinked and peered into the barn's dimness. "Smitty didn't seem like the screaming type to me. Let's hide a few minutes. Maybe we imagined the scream. Or maybe someone's trying to scare us."

We waited in silence. No more screams. But I stalled for more time.

"Let's explore the barn," I said. "Mom played here when she was our age. Hey! Look at that black cow. What a whopper!"

We leaned on a rough pine rail. We peered into the stall. The cow peered back.

"Maybe it's Finn's," Maria said.

"Naw," I said. "Kaleb said Finn has a calf. They're little. This critter must weigh a million pounds. Maria, let's climb to the hayloft. We can see the whole farm from up there. We'll be able to spot anyone who might have screamed."

I ran to a wooden ladder. It was nailed to the barn wall.

"I'll go first," I said.

Maria didn't argue. Splinters pricked my fingers as I clutched the ladder. But I didn't let on.

I paused, panting when I reached the hayloft. Maria followed on my heels. The hay door hung open. Dust mites drifted in the sunshine. I picked up a handful of prickly hay.

"What a clean, neat smell," I said. "Nothing like our Palace Apartment in New York."

Three pigeons flew out the hay door. A barn owl hooted from the rafters.

"Cody," Maria said. "See that heavy rope hanging by the door? Why's it moving? We didn't touch it."

Hair prickled on the back of my neck. Maria was right. The hay rope was swaying.

"Maybe the wind blew it," I said. "Or maybe a pigeon flapped against it."

But the wind wasn't blowing. And the pigeons hadn't flown near the rope. Mom hadn't told me the barn was so creepy.

Maria touched my arm. "I hear someone groaning," she said. "I'm getting out of here."

Maria hurried down the ladder. I followed her, missing the last two steps. We ran to the door and looked outside.

I whispered, "Someone's hiding behind those purple thistles."

"Be careful," Maria whispered as I stepped from the barn.

"We see you," I yelled. "Come on out!" I sounded braver than I felt.

Wow! A dark head appeared. A boy about my age limped forward.

He had black hair and high cheekbones. His eyes were like ebony buttons. He was an Indian! Where had he come from?

"Who are you?" I asked. "Why were you spying on us?"

"I have as much right here as you do," the boy said. He balanced on one leg like a stork.

"You're hurt!" Maria cried. She stepped forward. The boy hopped backward.

"Leave me alone!" he snapped. "I was here first. We don't need you here."

"You *live* here?" I asked. "What's your name?"

"Finn Webster," the boy said. "Who were you expecting?"

I shrugged. I hadn't expected Finn to be an Indian. Maria spoke up. "You jumped from the hayloft, didn't you? That's why the hay rope was moving. And you're hurt. Come with us, Finn. Cody's mom will help you."

"I don't need help," Finn growled.

"I suppose not," Maria said. "You're very brave."

Maria was always the peacemaker! How could she be so nice to this kid? It grossed me out.

And now she was offering Finn a cinnamon ball. I hated admitting it. But maybe I was a little bit jealous.

"You may not need us, Finn," Maria said. "But we need you. We have a lot of questions. Is that creature in the barn your calf?"

Some of Finn's anger disappeared. He took the cinnamon ball.

"Yes, it's my calf," Finn said. "Her name's Molly. She weighs about a thousand pounds—not a million. I've been feeding her all summer." Finn looked at me in disgust.

"You're pretty smart to raise such a neat calf," Maria said. "Come to lunch with us. Then you can tell us more about the farm."

"Did you hear a scream a while ago?" I asked. Drat it. We really did need Finn.

Finn scowled at me. "I suppose you think I was trying to scare you," he said. "It's not fair! When bad stuff happens, *I* always get blamed."

"What about the scream?" Maria asked.

"It came from the Bensons'," Finn said. "They live down the road a bit. Sometimes animals raid their turkey flock. So they rigged a recording of a scream. It goes off automatically now and then and scares animals away."

"It scared us too," Maria said.

"What's going on here?" Kaleb asked, joining us.

"Nothing," Maria and I said at the same time.

"Come with me, Finn." Kaleb motioned to Finn. "Let's wash for lunch."

We watched Finn tag after Kaleb. Then we went inside.

"Gram, we met Finn," I said. "He's prickly as a thistle. And he's an Indian!"

"Is that important?" Gram asked. Her blue eyes turned flint gray.

"No," I said. "I suppose not."

"Finn's father was Kaleb's son," Gram explained. "His mother was a full-blooded Sioux. Finn's parents died in a flash flood in Montana. Kaleb adopted Finn. And Finn enjoys the farm."

"Cody and Maria will enjoy having him here," Mom said.

"Good," Gram said. She tucked her pink shirt into her jeans. Then she bent over to retie one pink sneaker.

"Sometimes a person acts his worst when he needs friends the most. Please be kind to Finn."

Gram served fried green tomatoes for lunch. I held my breath and swallowed them. Would they be in her G cookbook? Or her T cookbook? She sure served weird food.

Finn was weird too. He didn't speak to anyone at lunch. He just ate and left.

I could hardly wait until lunch ended. I planned to study the treasure map as soon as we were finished eating.

But instead, Gram sent Maria and me to gather eggs. We searched the henhouse. Then we looked for nests in the barn.

A sudden movement startled us. Finn's dark clothing blended with the shadows. But I saw Finn struggling with Molly. They were in a narrow stall.

"Let me help," I said. I forced myself to be friendly. "I'll hold the stall door. You lead Molly through."

Finn nodded. He was still scowling.

A chicken startled Molly as I opened the door. She rolled her eyes. And she jerked from Finn's grasp.

I had to act quickly. Molly was about to smash Finn against the wall.

I propped the stall door open with a bucket. Then I grabbed Molly's halter. The tough leather stretched as I pulled. What if it snapped? Good-bye, Finn.

But Molly moved away from the wall. She headed into the barn. Shaking with relief, I ran to Finn.

"You okay?" I asked.

Finn limped off without saying a word.

"Not even a thank you," Maria said. "Some kid!"

"Don't rush him," I said. "I feel sorry for Finn now that I know more about him. I know how it is to lose a parent. And Finn's lost two."

Maria smiled at me. I liked that a lot.

We took the eggs to the kitchen. Then we went to the porch to study the treasure map.

"Look at this square," I said. I held the map toward Maria. "It's marked *windlass.*"

"What's a windlass?" Maria asked. "Do you suppose there's one around here somewhere?"

4

A Shovel for Digging

"Finn might know about a windlass," Maria said. "Let's go ask him."

We walked to Finn's cottage and knocked. Finn stood inside like a silent shadow.

"Finn, we have a treasure map," I said. "We want to find those missing emeralds."

"You're wasting your time," Finn said.

"You never know what you can do until you try," I said, smiling.

"KIDS FIND MISSING TREASURE!" Maria shouted.

Finn stepped outside. He almost returned Maria's smile.

"You think I can help?" he asked. He looked doubtful.

"We're looking for a windlass," I said. "What's a windlass?"

"It's a hoist, city boy. It's used to lift things," Finn explained. "Why do you care?"

I turned away. "Okay, so you don't want to help," I said. "We'll find it on our own."

"Wait," Finn said. He grabbed the map and studied it. "Is this map over ten years old?"

"Of course," Maria said. "Cody's uncle died 25 years ago. The police found it in his billfold."

Finn led us to a crumbling foundation. "Our cottage once sat right here," Finn said. "Ten years ago a tornado sucked it up like a cardboard box. The storm plunked it down where it is now."

"Awesome!" I said. I couldn't imagine such a storm. Was Finn lying?

"You can see the windlass from here," he said.

Maria and I followed Finn. He stopped at a tangle of honeysuckle vines. I took three deep breaths. I liked that sweet honeysuckle smell.

THE CASE OF THE MISSING EMERALDS

Finn pointed to a well and a rope. The rope was wrapped around a horizontal bar. Two vertical posts supported the bar.

Finn ignored the honeybees buzzing around the honeysuckle blossoms. He turned the rusty crank. It groaned. It squeaked. Then the bucket splashed into the water.

"We don't need this well now," Finn said. "Grandfather piped water to the cottage."

Finn scowled. "I saw you two snooping in the trees this morning."

"Were you spying on us?" I asked. "Why? We were only exploring. Have you met Smitty—I mean Professor Bidwell?"

"No," Finn said. "He's just another nosy outsider. What's next on your map?"

Is he really interested? I wondered. Or is he just avoiding talking about Smitty? "The map arrow points 50 yards to the east," I said. "Let's pace it off."

Maria took the map. "This U-shaped mark must be important," she said. "It must be the spot where something's hidden."

Finn and I matched strides. We began pacing. "Forty-eight. Forty-nine. Fifty!" I shouted. I glanced around, balancing on the last step. We were in the shadowed pine grove.

"What a crazy place to hide emeralds," I said.

"Nothing here but trees," Finn said. "Your map's a big phony."

"A treasure would be buried," I said. I studied the ground.

"So start digging," Finn invited.

"Do you have a shovel, Finn?" Maria asked.

"Yes," he said. "I'll get it for you."

"Great!" I said. "There's a compass in our car. I'll go get it. We need to find due east. Let's meet back here in five minutes."

Finn nodded. But he said nothing.

Finn strolled toward the barn. Maria and I dashed to the car. We found the compass. We paced off the distance carefully. Several points fell in line with due east.

"Look, Maria." I pointed. "See this indented place in the ground? Here's where I want to dig."

We sat down and waited. And waited. And waited.

"I think Finn's deserted us," Maria said. She finished her second cinnamon ball. "He's probably inside laughing. Cody, surely there's a shovel in Kaleb's toolshed."

"Good thinking," I said. We ran to the shed and found a spade.

Then we dashed back to the pine grove. I began digging. I also began sweating.

"Let me dig," Maria said. "Let's try another spot."

"No," I said. "Let's dig here a while longer. Emeralds would be buried deeply."

Just then the dinner bell clanged. We dropped the shovel. And we headed for the house.

31

THE CASE OF THE MISSING EMERALDS

Mom greeted us at the door. Then she pointed us to soap and water. We washed.

Kaleb and Finn arrived. Finn hardly said a word. I wasn't about to ask him why he left us waiting. I wouldn't let him know I cared.

Tonight Gram served corn on the cob. Yummy! I hoped she had a corn-on-the-cob cookbook. But that buttermilk! Yuck!

After supper, Mom spoke up. "First we'll clean up the kitchen," she said. "Then we're going to River Bluffs. The stores are open tonight. Everyone will be in town. We'll let folks know we've come to visit."

No one spoke. Mom's tone left no room for argument. And I was glad.

I wanted to see River Bluffs. I wanted to meet our future friends. Maybe Gram was wrong about people snubbing her.

"What will we do in town?" Maria asked.

"You can buy batteries for your radio," Mom said. "I know you've missed listening to your headset. And Cody needs a haircut. Gram can buy food for the pantry. I'm going to get gas for the car."

Gram refused to go. So Mom agreed to shop for groceries.

It was only a few miles to River Bluffs. Mom stopped at a service station outside town. Five old men lounged near a soda machine. A gasoline smell drifted through the car windows.

A train roared through town. The ground vibrated.

One man helped Mom pump the gas. The other four men walked toward the stores on Main Street.

"Be friendly to everyone," Mom urged. "And don't be surprised if people know your name. Strangers are big news. Those men went to spread the word. They'll tell people we're here."

Mom drove to Main Street. She parked near the barbershop. Then I got out of the car.

I saw lots of men in the barbershop. I stalled. I checked my billfold for money.

I listened to the sounds of the village. Rusty awnings squeaked. But they shaded the cracked cement sidewalks. Car tires crunched on loose gravel. Here and there laughter rang out.

At last, I gathered my courage. I eased into the shop. A path opened for me as if by magic.

The barber motioned me to his empty chair. He was tall and thin. His silver hair looked like a crown. I nicknamed him "The King."

Jeepers! All those guys weren't waiting for haircuts. They were just hanging out with their friends.

I climbed into the chair. It was like a black leather throne. The King pumped a lever. And the throne raised me up, up, and up.

The men didn't exactly stare. But I felt them studying me. I smiled at The King. Then I explained how I wanted my hair cut.

"I can tell you're a Cornwall, lad," The King said. "What's your name?"

"Cody," I said. "We're visiting Gram for the summer."

"How do you like it here?" The King asked. "It must be dull compared to New York City."

"Oh no, sir," I said. "I love the farm."

"Goldfinch Farm has always been an interesting place," The King said.

He clipped and snipped. Was there a hidden meaning in his words?

At last, he finished. I paid him and headed for our car. I stumbled just outside the door. And I couldn't help overhearing a man's words.

"Who do those Cornwalls think they are?" he asked. "They're bold as brass."

"Don't let them upset you," another voice replied. "They won't last the summer. Mind my words. They won't last the summer."

5

Prowler in the Night

I grabbed my billfold. I jammed it into my pocket. I wanted to run to the car. But I forced myself to walk.

"How did it go?" Mom asked.

"Everyone acted friendly while I was inside," I said. Then I repeated the ugly remarks I'd overheard. "I guess Gram wasn't kidding when she said people snubbed her. That's unfair, Mom. It's really rotten."

"Yes," Mom agreed. "It's unfair. I wish Great-grandfather hadn't decorated our house so elegantly. That started the rumors about the necklace."

"Everyone treated me just fine," Maria said. "They were out of batteries, so I bought cinnamon balls. I like River Bluffs. The clerk gave me a handbill advertising a fair. It sounds like fun. BLUE RIBBONS FOR EVERYONE!"

I glanced back as Mom drove away. The King and his subjects stared after us. I squirmed. I was even more convinced.

Winning friends here depended on finding the emeralds. Finding them and returning them to the Glockner family.

"I remember the fairs, Maria," Mom said. "The fair was *the* event of the summer. My brother and I always competed. We each tried to win the most blue ribbons."

"Let's drive around town before we leave," I said. "We've hardly seen any of it."

"You've seen the biggest part," Mom said. "The grain elevator dominates the north edge of town. The church spire reigns over the south side. I guess we could drive past the park."

Car tires crunched in the gravel. We passed the oak-shaded bandstand on the courthouse square. Soon we were in the country again. And Mom turned toward home.

I smelled the sweet scent of newly mowed hay. And I watched the moon rise. It was like a pumpkin glowing on the horizon. What a great ride home!

Gram met us at the back door. She served mugs of sassafras tea.

"How were things in town?" she asked.

"Fine," I said quickly. "People were friendly. And we found everything we needed." I didn't want Gram to know what I had overheard. That would just make it worse.

Did she know that her tea tasted like boiled grass? I didn't tell her. How lonely she must be out here. Maybe people weren't avoiding *her*. Maybe they were avoiding her buttermilk. And her boiled-grass tea.

"You should go with us next time," Mom said. "You'd enjoy it."

"Maybe we could go to the fair," Maria said. "CORNWALLS WIN SWEEPSTAKES. Mrs. Cornwall, why not enter something in the fair? They have divisions for canned goods."

"I used to enter my asparagus jelly," Gram said. "Years ago—before I let gossip defeat me."

Asparagus jelly? I tried not to gag. But my mouth filled with a slimy green taste.

"Let's all enter something this year," I said.

"Forget it," Maria said. "Entries must be something a person made or raised."

37

"Finn could enter Molly," Gram said. "I could enter my canned peas, but . . ."

"Do it, Gram," I said. "Do it."

Just then I heard a noise. It was sort of a scraping sound. It was close by.

I walked to the kitchen window. But I didn't see anyone outside. Yet something had to be there.

I smelled a tangy mint odor. Something had disturbed Gram's herb bed.

Later I made an excuse to go outside. I told Gram I wanted to see the moon again. But clouds had blown in. So there wasn't any moonlight.

I crept through the darkness. The mint patch grew right under the kitchen window. I didn't see anybody. I bent over and patted the ground. There! I felt trampled mint stalks.

I could still smell the strong, minty odor. Someone had lurked under the window. Someone had listened to our conversation.

I had no chance to talk to Maria until after breakfast. I motioned her to follow me. We went to the mint bed.

"I know someone was listening," I said. "Let's look for footprints."

"It's too dry for footprints," Maria said. "But it had to be Kaleb or Finn. Or it could have been the professor. There's nobody else around."

"Why would any of them be snooping?" I asked. "Smitty's here working on a book. He's not interested in our business. Kaleb often goes to town. He knows what goes on there."

"So that leaves Finn," Maria said. She stamped her foot at a chicken heading for the porch. "Nothing Finn does surprises me. He's weird."

"I'm going to talk to Finn right now," I said.

"You've no right to accuse him of spying," Maria said. "You'll just make him mad."

"I'm only going to talk to him," I said. "Maybe I'll ask him to enter Molly in the fair. He could represent Goldfinch Farm."

We ran to the barn, and I called to Finn.

"What do *you* want?" Finn asked. He glared at me.

"How's Molly's leg?" Maria asked.

Finn softened. He walked to the huge Angus. He examined the wound. I saw a red scar on Molly's black hide.

"It's healing," Finn said. "She caught her leg in the pasture fence. I saved her life."

"BOY SAVES HUGE BEAST!" Maria spouted her headline.

I doubted Finn's words. But I didn't argue.

"Why don't you show Molly at the fair?" I asked. "We'd like Goldfinch Farm to be represented. But Maria and I have nothing to enter."

"Molly isn't going to the fair," Finn said, scowling. "I want nothing to do with the people of River Bluffs."

"Why are you so bitter, Finn?" I asked. "Nobody

really likes being all alone. What's bugging you, anyway?"

"Nothing's bugging me," Finn snapped. "I have Grandfather and Molly. That's all the company I need."

"You must have some school friends," Maria said. "Are you in seventh grade?"

"I would be," Finn said. "But I'm not going back. No way."

"The law says you have to," I said.

"You'll miss a lot of fun if you don't go," Maria said.

"Huh!" Finn snorted. "You'd hate school, too, if kids called you dumb. And lazy. And if they taunted you about the emeralds. 'Ask Finn,' " he mimicked. " 'He's very wealthy.' "

"Why not try being friendly?" Maria asked. "The kids might treat you better. I don't think you're lazy or dumb. But you've snagged me on your barbs. Sometimes I feel like saying stuff I don't really mean because you make me mad."

"That's probably how it is with the school kids," I said.

Finn had no chance to reply. Gram called Maria and me to help in the garden. What a job!

We picked sweet corn. We picked green beans. Then we husked sweet corn for lunch. And we snapped the beans.

But this would be better than carrot soup. Or artichoke casserole. A lot better!

After lunch, we grabbed our shovel. We headed for the pine grove.

"Where was that hole we started digging?" Maria asked. "I don't see it."

"We left a mound of dirt," I said.

We slowed down and began searching carefully. "Did we come in the wrong direction?" I asked. "Let's go back to the edge of the grove."

"Let's try the directions again," Maria said. "We must have turned off course."

We retraced our steps. We saw familiar landmarks between the grove and the old well. We paced carefully between the trees.

"Maria!" I yelled. "Look at this!" I kicked some logs to one side. "What's been going on here?"

6

The Redwood Chest

The logs hid lots of loose earth.

"I think Finn did this," I said. "Let's talk to him."

Finn answered the door at the cottage. He was holding a baby pig.

"I'm busy," he said. "What do you want?"

"Why do you have a pig indoors?" Maria asked.

"It's the runt of a litter," Finn said. "I'm fattening it. Someday I'm going to be a veterinarian."

Finn sat on the doorstep. He fed the piglet from a baby bottle.

"BOY SAVES PIG," Maria said. She offered us cinnamon balls. Then she took one herself.

"Why did you fill our hole?" I asked. "And why did you hide the spot?"

"What hole?" Finn demanded.

"You know what hole," I said. "The one Maria and I dug in the grove. And why did you leave us waiting yesterday?"

"I meant to return," Finn said. "But Piggy was squealing. I stopped to feed it. I'll go back to the hole now if you want me to."

He placed the piglet in a box. Then he joined us.

We walked back to the grove. We kicked the logs aside. And we took turns digging. Before long we stopped to rest.

"How about entering Molly in the fair, Finn?" I asked. "You might get a blue ribbon. You'd show people that you've raised a first-class Angus."

"You mean it'd prove I'm not a lazy Indian?" Finn snorted.

"Cody didn't mean it that way," Maria said.

"Maria and I can enter the fair," I said. "*If* we find the emeralds."

"Emeralds at a fair?" Finn laughed at us.

I nodded. "There's an Unusual Exhibit category," I said.

"We have to find the emeralds first," Maria said. She began digging again.

I took over when she got tired. And hey! The shovel hit something hard.

Finn gasped. Maria stepped closer to the hole.

"It's probably a tree root," I said. I thrust the shovel again. Again it smashed into something hard.

"No," I said. "There's something here."

"Pull it up," Finn said.

"I can't get the shovel under it," I said.

We all began scooping dirt with our hands. Maria touched the object first.

"Here it is," she whispered. "Feel right here under my hand, Cody."

I began shoveling again. Soon we saw the top of a reddish brown box.

"KIDS FIND REDWOOD CHEST!" Maria shouted. But I shushed her.

"Keep quiet," I said. "Let's pull it up."

We scooped dirt. Finally, I got my hand under a corner of the chest. I lifted. Maria and Finn helped. And we had it.

The chest looked small out on level ground. Finn tapped it as if testing a melon for ripeness.

"Open it, Cody," Maria said. "Open it!"

"It's nailed shut," I said. "We need a pry bar."

"I brought a screwdriver from the shed," Maria said.

"It has to be the emeralds," I muttered. "What else could it be?"

I pried the chest open. We stood back, puzzled.

"Shucks!" Finn said. "I knew you wouldn't find emeralds."

"What is that thing?" Maria asked.

I ran my finger over a rough metal shaft. "It looks like a d-dagger," I said.

"I'm out of here!" Maria dashed toward the house. Finn ran close behind.

I slammed the top onto the chest. Then I sprinted after them. Finn disappeared into the barn.

"What's up, kids?" Mom asked when we reached the house.

"We found something terrible," I said.

"Shh," Mom said. "Don't upset your grandmother."

Bit by bit, Maria and I told our story.

"Now calm down, kids," Mom said. "There's probably a simple explanation. My brother never owned a dagger. And if he did, why would he bury it?"

I hated returning to the grove. But having Mom along gave me courage. After all, an old piece of metal couldn't hurt anyone. But seconds later, my stomach felt like an icebag.

We stepped into the shadowy grove. Some giant hand had pulled a dark veil across the sun. This time I hated the damp pine odor. It almost choked me.

"Which way, Cody?" Mom asked.

I trudged to the chest. But something was wrong. I'd replaced the chest lid. But now it lay on the ground.

"Is this your idea of a joke?" Mom asked. Her eyes flashed fire.

"It's gone," I shouted. "Mom, believe me! That chest had a dagger in it. Someone's stolen it!" A chill crept along the back of my neck.

"Cody," Mom said. "There's nobody around. Kaleb's in the field. I saw the professor across the creek."

"But we saw a dagger," Maria insisted.

"Impossible!" Mom said. "Take the chest to the barn. Refill that hole. Don't say a word about this to your grandmother. I don't want her upset over nothing."

"But why would someone bury an empty box?" I asked.

"You're letting your imagination run away with you," Mom said. "There's no dagger here. I don't want to hear any more about it."

Mom left and I sighed. "We'll have to figure this out for ourselves, Maria," I said. "Maybe Uncle Cody buried the emeralds in that chest. Maybe someone found them. Maybe they left the dagger to scare him."

"Why would he have buried the emeralds?" Maria asked. "He would have returned them to the owners. Surely he wanted to clear the family name."

"I can't figure it out," I said. We refilled the hole.

Then we carried the chest to the barn. I covered it with a mound of straw. We ran to the house.

The evening meal dragged. I concentrated on Gram's purple T-shirt and sneakers. That way I wouldn't blurt something about the dagger.

I forced down steamed okra. Some bread absorbed the slickness in my mouth. Could a guy become famous for eating health food?

I poured my buttermilk on a potted plant. Nobody saw me do it. But it left white curds on the black potting soil. Even plants don't like buttermilk.

"You children are very quiet," Gram said. "Perhaps you're overtired. You'd better go to bed early tonight."

I hated early bedtime. But I went upstairs with Maria. I knew who took the dagger—Finn. Nobody else could have done it.

My mind flashed thoughts like a rolling TV screen. I felt certain Finn had eavesdropped last night. He must have filled the first hole we dug. And I guessed Finn stole the dagger.

There was only one way to know for sure. I had to find that dagger. I set my alarm clock for two a.m. I slipped it under my pillow.

Should I tell Maria my plans? It would be nice to have company. I tiptoed to her room.

"There you go blaming Finn again," Maria argued. "Count me out. It'll be dark as a closet at two o'clock. You can't find anything in the dark."

"There'll be a full moon," I said. "Finn wouldn't dare take the dagger to his cottage. He'd hide it nearby."

"All right," Maria agreed reluctantly. "I hate to admit it, but Finn must be guilty. Wake me when you're ready to go."

I went to bed. I woke up startled when the alarm jangled. Outside, the wind howled under the eaves.

Maria surprised me by being ready to go. We crept downstairs to the back door.

We were about to step onto the back porch. Then lightning lit the kitchen. Thunder rattled the windows. And rain poured in silver sheets.

7

Weasel in the Kitchen

It rained for two days. Gram knocked on my door during the second afternoon. Even her yellow shirt and sneakers didn't brighten the day.

"Have you persuaded Finn to enter Molly at the fair?" Gram asked.

"He isn't interested," I said.

Gram sighed. "I guess I've set a bad example. I should be friendlier. I should reach out to people. Maybe I should spend less time writing cookbooks."

"Couldn't you just suddenly be friendly?" I asked.

"I'm not sure," Gram answered. "I've considered donating land for a park. But right now, I'm concerned about Finn. He needs to meet kids his age. Maybe talking to him might change his thinking."

"Maybe," I said. I didn't want to talk to Finn. I thought he stole our dagger.

"Bring him to my room after supper," Gram said. "We'll work from there."

I sighed after Gram left. How could I get Finn to her room?

Finally, I had an idea. Finn wanted to be a veterinarian. I found a book on animal care on the bookcase.

After supper, I showed Finn the book. "You might like this, Finn," I said. "Let's ask Gram if you can borrow it."

Finn hesitated. Then he followed me. Gram smiled when we knocked on her door.

"Gram," I said, "I told Finn that you might lend him this book."

"Of course, Finn," Gram said. "You have a special way with animals."

She pushed two bowls toward us. "You boys didn't eat much dessert tonight. How about an apple?"

I hesitated. What was Gram up to now?

"Take your choice," she said. "The apples in the red dish are bruised. But these in the blue bowl are top quality. Look at them."

I took an apple. Finn chose one too.

"See the tiny hail marks on the skins?" Gram asked. "They grew in prime fruit country. The orchards there are high in the mountains where sudden storms rage."

Big deal, I thought. Why the lecture on apples? But an apple would taste better than gooseberry sauce.

That had been our dessert. Green gooseberry sauce! My mouth still puckered.

"Finn, have you considered entering Molly at the fair?" Gram asked.

"No." Finn's voice was flat as a slap.

"Better reconsider," Gram said. "You'd meet children your age."

"Huh!" Finn said. "They call me dumb and lazy."

"Silly ideas float all around us," Gram said. "Some folks believe that certain races are inferior. They judge people by the color of their skin. Thinking people know better."

"I hate it when the kids call me names," Finn said.

"They're just repeating false ideas they've heard," Gram said. "Be friendly, Finn. But friendliness alone isn't enough. You have to write your own price tag."

"Price tag?" Finn asked.

"Which bowl of apples did you choose from?" Gram asked.

"The blue," Finn replied. "You said they were best."

"Examine them, boys," Gram said. "All the apples are the same."

Finn and I looked at the apples. All of them had tiny hail marks.

"I wrote a price tag on the apples," Gram said. "It's how you feel about the hail marks that's important. Do they prove the apples are inferior? Or do they prove the apples came from a superior fruit-growing district? It's all how you look at it."

"But they're all the same," I said.

"But I made you think some were better than others because they came from different places," Gram explained.

"I'm beginning to understand," Finn said. "My skin is dark. But I'm proud of my Indian blood. And I'm as good as anyone else."

"Good," Gram said. "Write your price tag high. The color of your dreams and thoughts is important. Dreams and thoughts are more important than the color of your skin. Once you believe that, others will believe it also."

"Why not enter Molly in the fair?" I asked.

"I'm entering some needlework," Gram said.

"I'd like to read this book," Finn said. He took the book and left.

Nothing was settled. But I knew that Finn had new ideas to consider. So did I.

The rain stopped the next morning. But the wind continued. And clouds masked the sun.

Maria and I watched Finn. He led Molly in circles in the pasture.

"Gram says that owners lead their calves before the fair judges," I explained. "Molly must get used to the rope and halter."

"Then Finn must be training Molly for the fair," Maria said. We walked to the pasture fence. But Finn ignored us.

"Guilty conscience," Maria said. "He hid that dagger. Now he hates facing us."

"Maybe Finn didn't take it," I said. "Maybe Smitty knows something about that dagger. Let's go see him. Let's nose around."

We hurried through the dusky grove. The swollen stream glistened and gurgled in the meadow. We waded across. The icy water numbed our legs.

"Hello, kids." Smitty called. "Pull up a stump and sit down." He stood up. A paper fluttered to the ground.

I saw telltale lines of a map. Smitty grabbed the paper. He tucked it into his notebook.

Somehow I didn't like him so much anymore. Cancel the nickname. From now on, he was just Professor Bidwell. Why was he hiding a map from us?

"What did you kids do during the rain?" he asked.

"We helped Gram around the house," I said.

Then I changed the subject. "Maria and I have lost a toy dagger." I held up my hands to show the size.

I watched the professor's reaction carefully. "Finn may have hidden it. Have you seen it?"

"No," Professor Bidwell said. "But if I do, I'll let you know."

We talked for a few moments. Then Maria spoke. "We'd better leave now. It was nice seeing you again."

I watched the professor. I saw him studying the map he'd tucked out of sight.

"Maria, why would he make a map?" I asked. "Maybe he *is* searching for the emeralds."

"Maybe," Maria said. "I'm glad you told him the dagger was a toy."

Clouds hid the sun. But the air was hot and muggy. The day turned into a steam oven. Gram made a pitcher of lemonade to cool us off.

"Cody, will you and Maria please carry this to Kaleb?" Gram handed me a glass of lemonade. "He'll soon be in from the field. He'll welcome something cool."

"Sure," I said. But it bugged me. Finn was right there. Why couldn't he do it?

But I didn't complain. I took the glass, and Maria and I went to find Kaleb. Finn followed. At Finn's cottage, the door hung open.

I jumped as we stepped inside. I was startled by a streak of dark fur darting toward the kitchen.

"What was *that*?" Maria asked. "It was too big for a mouse—or even a r-rat."

"It looked like a weasel," Finn said, joining us. "They usually prowl at night. But I've had an injured chicken in here. Old weasel must have smelled it. Let's leave the door open. We can scare it back outside."

We searched carefully inside all the cupboards. We couldn't find the weasel.

"What about that door under the sink?" I asked. "It's nailed shut."

"Nothing there," Finn said. "There's just an opening that lets Grandfather reach the plumbing pipes."

"The weasel doesn't know that," I said. "Let's open it."

Finn found a claw hammer. And we pried the door open. The weasel tore from its hiding place. It escaped through the front door.

"Wow!" Maria said. "What a scare!"

I agreed. Then something caught my eye. I dropped to my knees.

I peered inside the cupboard. There was the missing dagger! I saw it wedged behind the plumbing pipes.

8

Tornado

I stared at the dagger. Finn looked surprised too. So did Maria. She was even too surprised to blurt a headline.

"Maria, run get Mom," I said. "Now she'll have to believe us. Finn and I will stay here and guard this thing."

Maria dashed off. In moments she returned with both Mom and Kaleb.

"Mom," I said. "Now do you believe us? It's a dagger, right?"

"It seems to be," Mom replied. "But where did it come from? Why would my brother have buried it?"

"I can explain," Kaleb said.

"Then please do," Mom said. "We must call the police if there's been a crime."

Kaleb removed his straw hat and twisted it nervously. "It's a long-ago story," Kaleb said. "The police found a map after your brother's accident. Your mother thought it might lead to the emeralds. But the police found nothing. So later, I followed the map. I found this dagger."

"In the redwood chest?" I asked. "We put the chest in the barn for safekeeping."

"No, the dagger wasn't in the chest," Kaleb said. "It lay loose in the ground. I hated thinking of what it might mean."

There was complete silence as we listened to Kaleb's story.

"Young Cody had a hot temper," Kaleb went on. "Kids teased him about his fine home. And about the missing emeralds. I was afraid his anger might have led him to trouble. Had he committed a crime? Had he tried to hide the evidence? Those were my first worries."

"I can understand that," Mom said.

Kaleb continued. "Then I thought he might have planned some future crime. He had a weapon ready. That was a scary thought too."

"So what did you do?" I asked.

"I hid the dagger in that redwood chest," Kaleb said. "Then I reburied it. Your uncle was dead. I hoped I'd never have reason to dig up the dagger."

"Did you think about going to the police?" Maria asked.

"Not unless I had to," Kaleb said. "Mrs. Cornwall was grieving over her son's death. We didn't need any more problems. I watched the newspapers. But I saw nothing about unsolved crimes. So I kept quiet."

"Then *you* filled in the first hole we dug," Cody said. "Before we found the chest."

"Yes." Kaleb flushed. "I hoped you'd forget about more digging. I should have dug up the chest right then. I should have hidden it where you couldn't find it."

"Why didn't you?" I asked.

"I was busy with chores," Kaleb said. "That night, I listened outside the kitchen window. Nobody mentioned the dagger. I felt relieved. But I planned to move it later after Finn went to bed.

"But that plan failed," Kaleb continued. "Finn had a sick piglet in the house. He was up and down all night taking care of it. He would have been suspicious if I had left the cottage during the night."

"So we found the dagger before you could move it," I said. "Finn, I owe you an apology. I was blaming you for taking it."

58

"I was returning from the field when you found the dagger," Kaleb said. "I took it when you ran to the house to get your mother. I hoped to hide that dagger where you'd never find it. If it hadn't been for that weasel . . ."

"I'm sorry, Kaleb," Mom said. "But we'll have to report this to the police. Even after all these years. If my brother committed some crime, we'll have to face up to it."

What a bummer! I had tried to find the emeralds. I wanted to clear the family name. I wanted Gram to be happier in River Bluffs.

But I'd only caused trouble. I really felt bad.

"We'll drive to the police station," Mom said. "We'll have to tell Mother first. I hate having to upset her over this."

We all looked out the window. What was that roar? It sounded like a train approaching. But we weren't near any train tracks.

The darkness outside surprised me. It was only midafternoon.

I stepped onto the front porch. Straw and leaves were whirling in the wind. The sky was the color of lead. Greenish clouds quivered above us like giant mounds of spoiled Jell-O.

"Run for the storm cellar!" Kaleb shouted. "It's a tornado!"

Kaleb and Finn dashed toward the cellar. They

dodged branches that hurtled through the air like missiles. Mom tugged Maria and me toward safety. Gram ran from the house and joined us.

Finn and I opened the cellar door. Kaleb helped until everyone slipped inside. The door banged shut. Total darkness swallowed us.

Nobody spoke. I hated the musty smell of the cellar. My wet shirt and jeans clung to my skin. Water dripped into my sneakers.

I felt around in the dark. I found the shelves that held Gram's canned goods. I grabbed for support.

"We're mighty lucky to be in here," Kaleb said at last. "Mighty lucky! It's the safest place to be in a twister. Sure hope that funnel misses the farm."

"Funnel?" Maria asked. Her voice shook. I guessed she was too scared to create a headline.

"A tornado cloud's called a funnel," Kaleb said. "The wind rushes round and around. It finally forms a funnel-shaped cloud. I saw it high in the sky to the southwest."

"Sometimes the wind blows more than 300 miles an hour," Finn said.

"What if the house blows away?" I asked. "You said your cottage blew away one time."

"Let's save our worrying," Mom said. "Maybe everything will be okay. These windstorms are violent. But they move fast. The funnel may not touch ground anywhere near here."

I recognized Mom's store-detective tone. I knew she was trying to keep us calm.

"There are candles and matches on one of the shelves," Gram said. "Find them. We can have a bit of light. But mind now. Be careful of my jars."

I ran my hand along one rough, dusty shelf. I was starting to explore another. Then Finn let out a whoop.

"Here they are!" Finn cried. "Matches. I have them." In a moment, a match flared. I smelled sulfur. Then a candle glowed.

Eerie light sent fluttering shadows quivering into dusky corners. I lit another candle—and another. A flickering dimness bathed the whole cellar.

The air grew warm and close. Kaleb pushed on the door to try to let in some fresh air. But the pressure from outside forced it shut.

There was nothing to do but wait. It was like being in a corked jug. I crawled onto a shelf with some smelly onions. That made more room for the others.

"I wonder if Professor Bidwell is safe," I said.

"He'll probably lose his tent," Kaleb guessed. "But he's smart. He'll lie in a ditch or some low spot. He'll be okay."

The wailing and lashing of the storm lessened. Kaleb tried the door again. It opened just a crack. I could hardly believe what I saw.

9

Trapped!

I'd never seen it rain so hard before. It was like a ghostly hand had turned on a million faucets. But I liked the way the fresh air cooled my hot cheeks.

"The worst of the storm has passed," Kaleb said. He peered into the rain. "The house is still standing. But many trees are down. I can't see the cottage from here."

I hoped the cottage was all right. But I wouldn't care if the dagger had been blown away. I held my breath as Mom looked at Gram and started to talk.

"Mother," Mom began. "Did my brother own a dagger?"

"Not that I ever knew about, Gwen," Gram said. "Why do you ask?"

Mom repeated the story about the dagger—and about the redwood chest. Gram listened without interrupting. But she moved closer to the door as if she needed more air.

"That's hard to believe, Gwen," Gram said. "Your brother never got along with the townspeople. But there was never any violence around River Bluffs. At least not that I can remember. Never!"

"There's probably nothing to fear," Mom said. "We'll check with the police once it's safe to leave here."

"We can make it right now," Kaleb said. "The rain's let up. And the wind's died down to a breeze."

One by one, we crept from the cellar. Then we headed for the house. I helped Gram over fallen branches and around puddles.

"What a mess!" I said.

"THE SKY HAS FALLEN!" Maria shouted. "FAMILY ESCAPES TORNADO!"

Sticks and straw littered the farmyard. Branches lay everywhere. And a huge elm sprawled like a fallen giant across the driveway.

Shattered glass glittered on the back porch. The clothesline dangled like a piece of cooked spaghetti. But Kaleb's cottage was okay.

"Mom!" I pointed to the blocked driveway. "We're trapped here."

"Try the phone," Gram said.

I moved carefully through broken glass and went inside. I grabbed the telephone receiver. But I knew in a second that the line was dead. That's when I remembered that the battery in the cell phone was dead.

"I'll get my chain saw," Kaleb said. "I'll cut the tree into smaller pieces. Then we can move them and get to the car. Come with me, Finn."

"Mom," I said. "May I go see if the professor needs help?"

"Yes," Mom said. "But take care."

"I'll go too," Maria said as Mom gave permission. "PROFESSOR SAVED BY CHILDREN!"

We stopped at the cottage. But Finn refused to join us.

"At least that makes one thing more simple," I said. We had left the dagger on the porch chair when the storm hit. Now I grabbed it when Finn and Kaleb weren't looking.

"What are you going to do?" Maria asked. "Why take the dagger?"

"That's my secret," I said. I found a paper sack and

hid the dagger inside it. "I have an idea that might solve some riddles around here."

"I'm not going anywhere with that dagger," Maria said.

"Okay," I said. "But keep my secret until I get back. Will you?"

Maria nodded, but she didn't move. I trotted toward the pine grove. My sneakers were already wet as sponges. So I splashed right into the creek.

I hurried to the spot where the professor's tent had been. Yikes! Suddenly I felt very cold. And very alone.

The tent hung wrapped around a pine tree. Camping equipment littered the ground. And Professor Bidwell was missing.

"Professor!" I shouted. "Professor! Do you hear me?" I listened without moving until I heard a voice. I tripped over branches and stumps.

But I finally reached the spot where the professor lay. A fallen pine tree pinned him to the ground.

"Maybe I can lift the tree," I said. But I knew I couldn't.

"No." The professor's voice wavered in pain. "Don't try. It's too heavy for you. I think my leg's broken. Please go for help."

I ran back to the house. I told Mom what I'd seen.

"Cody, you and Maria go tell Professor Bidwell that help's coming," Mom said.

It surprised me when Finn joined us. He brought a blanket and a thermos. We soon reached the professor's side. And Finn covered him with the blanket.

"Why cover him on such a hot day?" Maria asked.

"To prevent shock," Finn said. "I learned that from caring for animals." Finn helped the professor take a drink.

I waited until the professor seemed calm. Then I showed him the dagger. We kept quiet while he examined it.

"Where did you find this?" the professor asked. "Where? Where?" He tried to get up.

Then he sank back with a groan. "Tell me about the dagger, Cody."

I repeated the long story. "Mom's going to take it to the police after Kaleb clears the driveway."

"No!" the professor said. "No. Never. Hide it!"

What was going on here? I couldn't ask questions now. Kaleb and Mom had arrived.

"I'll lift up on the tree," Kaleb said. "Someone try to pull him from under it."

"No!" Finn cried. "It's never safe to move an injured person. It could cause more damage."

"The boy's right," the professor said.

"I'll run to town for a doctor," Finn said. "It's a long way, but . . ."

"The driveway's blocked," Kaleb explained to the

professor. "Finn's a good boy. He'll have help here soon."

"I'll give him a note so the doctor will believe him," Mom said. She tore a scrap from our paper sack. Then she looked inside the sack.

"Cody!" Mom shouted. "What's the meaning of this?"

"Don't scold him," Professor Bidwell said. "And don't be frightened. Give me time to talk to my coworker, Dr. Kellogg. He's at the university. We may be able to explain about the dagger."

"I want an explanation right now," Mom said. "Did you know my brother?"

"No," Professor Bidwell said. "Please call Dr. Kellogg. But don't tell him about the dagger. He's the head of my department. I'm not free to speak of this without his consent."

He told us how to contact Dr. Kellogg. "Tell him I need him," the professor said. "He'll drive here immediately."

"All right," Mom said. "But it will take a while to find a telephone. Cody, I'll deal with you later. You have a lot of explaining to do." Mom headed back toward the house.

Maria sat on a stump. I leaned against a tree. We talked to Professor Bidwell. We tried to keep him alert. But he scared me.

Why had he been afraid of the police? Why hadn't he wanted Dr. Kellogg to know about the dagger?

Was this guy a phony? Maybe he was a thief. Maybe he wanted the emeralds. Maybe he was a scam artist. Maybe he had a plan that would ruin us. Angry questions buzzed in my head like hornets.

Could Dr. Kellogg be Professor Bidwell's accomplice? What if the criminals trapped us on the farm?

I'd only wanted to return the emeralds to their owners. Did Professor Bidwell want the emeralds for himself? He could probably get rich by selling them.

I sighed. Now I had caused more trouble. Maybe I had pushed a thief into action.

I liked Gram. And I liked the farm. But Gram probably wouldn't invite us back here anytime soon.

10

A Surprising Situation

The minutes crawled like snails. But finally we heard voices.

"It must be the doctor," Maria said. "I'll check."

Seconds later, Maria returned. Something was wrong. Her eyes were as big as donut holes.

"Cody!" she cried. "It's the police!"

69

THE CASE OF THE MISSING EMERALDS

A jeep crashed through the trees. And two policemen jumped out. They introduced themselves—Sergeant Cade and Officer Dugan.

"This is Professor Bidwell." I introduced the men.

"We'll get him to the house," Sergeant Cade said. "Dr. Jackson's on his way. I'm certified to help the ambulance crew. But the ambulance is in use because of the tornado."

The officers placed the professor on a stretcher. Then they lifted him into the jeep. Maria and I squeezed in too. We headed for the house.

I dreaded facing Mom. Now I'd have to explain about taking the dagger to the professor.

At the house, Mom and Kaleb were clearing the driveway. I was in luck—for a while at least.

Gram sent Maria and me back to the grove. We needed to find the professor's laptop computer. He also wanted his papers and notebooks.

Should we walk slowly? That would delay my explanation to Mom. Or should we run? I wanted to know what was happening at the house.

"KIDS FIND VALUABLE COMPUTER!" Maria shouted. And we ran.

The laptop lay near the tent. Papers and notebooks were scattered everywhere. It took a long time to find everything.

"Hurry, Cody," Maria said.

Couldn't she see I was hurrying? I knew we were missing out on important stuff.

But we couldn't run back to the house. We were carrying too many things. We walked as quickly as we could.

We hurried inside. Gram took the things we'd found. We hurried into the parlor.

Everyone was crowded around the professor. He was lying on the parlor sofa. Dr. Jackson was examining him.

"No fractures," the doctor said. "Give him plenty of rest for a few days."

The doctor cleaned and bandaged the professor's leg. He left him some pain pills.

Gram gave the doctor a box of her asparagus cookies. A treat? Or a treatment? I wondered.

Gram also gave him special thanks. He usually didn't make house calls. Especially not out in the country. I guessed he was glad to get back to town.

Now Mom was on my case.

"Cody, we have some matters to discuss," she said. "In private."

My mouth went dry as an old sock. But I followed Mom to the dining room. "Mom, I was just trying to . . ." A knock interrupted us. Gram opened the door to a stranger.

"Dr. Kellogg?" Gram asked. "I'm Lucy Cornwall. Do come in."

Dr. Kellogg didn't look like a thief. I breathed easier. He looked a lot like Santa Claus. He was plump with red cheeks and silver-white hair. And his eyes twinkled when he smiled.

Gram shooed us from the parlor.

"Give the scholars privacy," she said.

Rats, I thought. Now Mom could question me again! But no. Again, I lucked out.

Dr. Kellogg reappeared. He asked for the dagger.

Gram brought him the weapon. He pulled it from the paper sack and examined it carefully. Then he invited everyone into the parlor.

"You have a rare find here," Dr. Kellogg began. "This copper dagger is very old. It will be of great value to scientists. It may have belonged to one of this area's earliest people."

"Cody!" Mom looked at me in surprise. "You must have guessed this all along."

"Oh no," I said. "But I did read some of Uncle Cody's books. I knew he must have been interested in ancient people. That gave me some ideas. I took the dagger to Professor Bidwell for his opinion."

"I'm glad you did that, Cody," the professor said. "One archaeological find usually leads to another."

The professor looked at Gram. "Would you allow the university to fence off that pine grove? Would you allow students to come here to dig?"

"I'll be happy to help," Gram said. "But why fence

the area? It's very private back here."

"Curious people flock to archaeological digs," Professor Bidwell said. "Everyone wants to find a treasure. A fence will protect the area."

"So that's why you wanted to see the dagger before we called the police," I said. "You scared me. I thought you might be a criminal. I thought you might be searching for the missing emeralds."

"I was trying to avoid the public," the professor explained. "Amateurs can ruin a valuable spot. Archaeological diggers need careful supervision. I want this spot saved for scientists."

"Maybe Uncle Cody planned to get professional help to dig," I said. "Maybe he buried the dagger to keep it safe. I'm guessing that's why he made a map. Then he died before he could tell anyone what he'd found."

"I've been thinking of donating some land to the Civic Club," Gram said. "For a park, perhaps. A fence would keep your site safe. People might like to come to a picnic area out this way."

"I'm sure they would," the professor agreed. "Your farm may become a scientific landmark."

I wondered if the park might rate a bronze marker. But I didn't ask.

"Professor," I said, "could we exhibit this dagger at the fair? I think people would like to see it up close."

"Good idea, Cody," the professor agreed. "Do you

like to write? You might write a few paragraphs to explain the exhibit. I'd be glad to help you."

We all talked and planned for a long time. At last, Dr. Kellogg left. Gram went to prepare a room for Professor Bidwell. Then Finn spoke up.

"Goldfinch Farm will have two entries at the fair," Finn said. "I want to enter Molly."

"Great," I said. "What made you change your mind?"

"My trip to get the doctor," Finn said. "One lady gave me a ride into River Bluffs. And three men went out of their way to help me find a doctor."

"That's cool," I said. "But what does that have to do with Molly and the fair?"

"Those people showed me I was wrong about River Bluffs," Finn said. "I've never done anything for them. Yet they helped me when I needed them."

"People can be like that," Mom said.

"I'd like to return the favor," Finn said. "I may not win a blue ribbon. But I'll never know what I can do until I try."

I caught Finn's teasing tone. He was repeating one of my favorite lines.

Laughter rang out. Everyone congratulated Finn.

Then Mom spoke. "Cody, are you terribly disappointed about failing to find the emeralds?"

"No," I said. "Okay, so I'm a little disappointed.

But the treasure I found may be more valuable than emeralds. Maybe people will forget gossip from the past."

"BOY SUCCEEDS BY FAILING," Maria said. Now that's a real headline.

That night, I could hardly sleep. Goldfinch Farm would attract people from all over the state. I might not be famous. I might not get my name on a bronze plaque. But fame wasn't everything.

People like me could do important things—even though we weren't famous. I'd found a bit of history to share with others. That history would be important for years to come.

I'd also found a way to help Gram make friends. Perhaps I'd been a good emissary after all.

As for fame—there's always tomorrow.